I · Thee · Wed

To _____

From _____

The moment two young people have made the mutual confession that their supreme happiness is wrapped up in each other, they are within measurable distance of the great crisis of their lives.

—Christine Terhune Herrick
The Modern Hostess
1908

I·Thee·Wed

The Sweet Nellie Book of
Wedding Traditions & Sentiments

PAT ROSS

V
VIKING
STUDIO
BOOKS

VIKING STUDIO BOOKS
Published by the Penguin Group
Viking Penguin, a division of Penguin Books USA Inc.,
375 Hudson Street, New York, New York 10014, U.S.A.
Penguin Books Ltd, 27 Wrights Lane, London W8 5TZ, England
Penguin Books Australia Ltd, Ringwood, Victoria, Australia
Penguin Books Canada Ltd, 2801 John Street, Markham, Ontario, Canada L3R 1B4
Penguin Books (N.Z.) Ltd, 182–190 Wairau Road, Auckland 10, New Zealand

Penguin Books Ltd, Registered Offices: Harmondsworth, Middlesex, England

First published in 1991 by Viking Penguin, a division of Penguin Books USA Inc.

1   3   5   7   9   10   8   6   4   2

Grateful acknowledgment is made to The Bettmann Archive for permission
to reproduce material from their collection.

LIBRARY OF CONGRESS CATALOGING IN PUBLICATION DATA
Ross, Pat
I thee wed : the Sweet Nellie book of wedding traditions &
sentiments / by Pat Ross.
p.   cm.
ISBN 0-670-83529-3
1. Marriage — Quotations, maxims, etc.   I. Title.
PN6084.M3R67   1991
392'.5 — dc20   90-55263

Printed in Japan   Set in Nicholas Cochin
Designed by Amy Hill

AN APPRECIATION

With the publication of each new book, there are new friends to thank and old friends to thank once again. My family's willingness to lend their many wonderful antique etiquette and entertainment books continues to enrich this group of diminutive treasures. I especially wish to thank my mother, Anita Kienzle, for allowing me to remove from their frames a Reinthal & Newman postcard series on courtship and marriage that my grandmother Jennie Welsh had collected.

Appreciation, as always, goes to Leisa Crane, for her research and cheerful availability, and to the enthusiastic and supportive staff at my shop, publisher, and literary agency, this stellar group including: Debbie Berbusse at Sweet Nellie; Barbara Williams, Michael Fragnito, Gerry Visco, and Amy Hill at Viking Studio Books; and Amy Berkower and Sheila Callahan at Writers House.

Patti O'Shaughnessy's special interest in this subject was certainly appreciated. Ingrid Savage and Diane Glenn came to the rescue with their lively ideas and antique books and papers. Susan Quick lived up to her name as she sorted through the details and typed all those quotations—so many reluctant runners-up in the file!

Erica and Joel continue to be my loved and loving supporters. My personal enthusiasm for this series is, happily, backed up by many well-wishers who remain unnamed here, but remembered.

INTRODUCTION

The idea for a book about wedding traditions occurred to me as I was elbow-deep in a box of antique lace that I'd "won" at an auction: the entire lot, sight unseen, went to the highest bidder. I had just discovered a bundle of lace carefully tied with satin ribbon—the exquisite trimmings from some bridal gown, perhaps—a veritable celebration of pattern, pearlwork, and other treasured handwork from years past. Someone had snipped the lace cuffs, collar, and other decorative trim from dress fabric so delicate that only wisps of silk remained attached to the lace. Perhaps the vintage scraps were saved for a new generation of brides, perhaps as a memento of a special day. I suddenly felt that I had wandered into someone else's memories.

Just as we have countless books and magazines offering advice on everything from bridal attire to the shape of the cake, our ancestors also consulted a variety of wedding experts. Rules of etiquette and advice from the nineteenth and early twentieth centuries, though often overflowing with propriety we find excessive by today's standards, still speak a language that translates well a century later. We still pledge love, present tokens of affection, take vows, and celebrate with enthusiastic pomp and circumstance that would make our ancestors proud. If anything, formal weddings are more popular than ever.

I was married in the 1960s in a mini-dress, a perfectly beautiful and traditional gown-and-veil ensemble—traditional except for the length, of course. My family had my official bridal picture cropped just above the hemline and then framed, my personal statement as an independent woman no longer an obvious breach of tradition. But I still have the uncensored version . . .

Now there is a welcome variety of wedding traditions, so that the past and present meet in the middle. We'll continue to fill our albums, press our flowers, treasure every memory, and, hopefully, save our lace to remind us of a day that is filled with tender emotions and lasting memories.

Love and Marriage

Some people fall in love with the swiftness and force of an electric shock, while with others the process is so gradual that the fact is not discovered until some accident or emergency reveals it to the interior perception.

—Jennie June
Talks on Women's Topics
1864

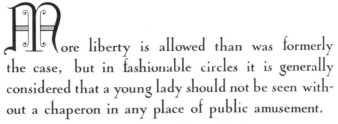

More liberty is allowed than was formerly the case, but in fashionable circles it is generally considered that a young lady should not be seen without a chaperon in any place of public amusement.

—Margaret E. Sangster
Good Manners for All Occasions
1904

Somebody at my elbow suggests that I have not intimated how a man should propose. The plain truth is I do not know. But a man must not be abject. Faint heart never won fair lady since the world began.

—Margaret E. Sangster
*Good Manners for
All Occasions*
1904

As I and you perhaps would do,
They gazed upon the ground;
But when they'd gone a yard or two
Of course they both looked round.

Perhaps there is such a thing as love at first sight, but love alone is a very uncertain foundation upon which to base marriage. There should be thorough acquaintanceship and a certain knowledge of harmony of tastes and temperaments before matrimony is ventured.

—*Our Deportment: Or The Manners, Conduct
and Dress of the Most Refined Society*
Compiled by John H. Young
1879

If their great aim and object be to marry, for pity's sake disguise it. It is disgusting to see it trotted out on every occasion; besides which, it utterly defeats its own purpose.

—Jennie June
Talks on Women's Topics
1864

Some young ladies think it smart to encourage a proposal and then refuse it. This is not a sign of good breeding; besides, her motives will soon become generally known, and she will be regarded as a "flirt."

—A. E. Davis
American Etiquette and Rules of Politeness
1882

But granting that a young man and a young woman love one another, have health, have courage and honor, they need not be deterred from marrying because they have little money. The very smallest income that may be depended upon will do as a beginning.

—Margaret E. Sangster
Good Manners for All Occasions
1904

COPYRIGHT 1905 THE ULLMAN MFG. CO. N.Y.

POPPING THE QUESTION

The wedding-ring, symbolical of the conjugal relation, has ever been the accepted accompaniment of marriage. Its being put on the fourth finger of the left hand has been continued, from long-established usage, because of the fanciful conceit that from this finger a nerve went direct to the heart.

—Frederick Saunders
*Salad for the Solitary
and the Social*
1871

MARRIAGE COMPARED WITH SINGLE LIFE.

Marriage is the proper scene of piety and
patience of the duty of parents and the charity
of relations : here kindness is spread abroad
and love is united and made firm as a centre.
Marriage is the nursery of Heaven.

Sensible

Advice

As we should say to women who wish for domestic happiness, never marry a pleasure-seeker, an idle man, so we would say to men, never marry any but an intelligent woman, for after purity, quite the next best thing is that good sense which comes with intelligence. It is the best of dowries.

—Mrs. H. O. Ward
Sensible Etiquette of the Best Society
1878

Wives who wish to retain their husbands as lovers must never indulge in fits of temper, hysterics, or other habits, which, easy to conquer in the outset, grow and strengthen with indulgence. Equally important is it that husbands should control their tempers and their tongues, and always leave home with loving words, and return to it with pleasant greetings.

—Mrs. H. O. Ward
Sensible Etiquette of the Best Society
1878

Respect for each other is as necessary to a happy marriage as that the husband and wife should have an affection for one another.

—*Our Deportment: Or The Manners, Conduct and Dress of the Most Refined Society*
Compiled by John H. Young
1879

All airs of mastership, all foolish display of jealousy, should be avoided. . . . Quarrels cannot but impair mutual respect and diminish love.

—*Good Manners: A Manual of Etiquette in Good Society*
1870

Marriage must exemplify friendship's highest ideal, or else it will be a failure.

—Margaret E. Sangster
Good Manners for All Occasions
1904

If husbands and wives generally would render each other half of the little attentions they lavished upon each other before marriage, their mutual happiness would be more than doubled.

—*Practical Etiquette*
1881

It is the heart and mind, not the pretty face, that endear a wife to her husband.

—*Practical Etiquette*
1881

Gathered Together

JANUARY	FEBRUARY
S - 4 11 18 25	S 1 8 15 22 ..
M - 5 12 19 26	M 2 9 16 23 ..
T .. 6 13 20 27	T 3 10 17 24 ..
W - 7 14 21 28	W 4 11 18 25 ..
T 1 8 15 22 29	T 5 12 19 26 ..
F 2 9 16 23 30	F 6 13 20 27 ..
S 3 10 17 24 31	S 7 14 21 28 ..

MARCH	APRIL
S 1 8 15 22 29	S .. 5 12 19 26
M 2 9 16 23 30	M - 6 13 20 27
T 3 10 17 24 31	T - 7 14 21 28
W 4 11 18 25 ..	W 1 8 15 22 29
T 5 12 19 26 ..	T 2 9 16 23 30
F 6 13 20 27 ..	F 3 10 17 24 ..
S 7 14 21 28 ..	S 4 11 18 25 ..

MAY	JUNE
S 3 10 17 24 31	S .. 7 14 21 28
M 4 11 18 25 ..	M 1 8 15 22 29
T 5 12 19 26 ..	T 2 9 16 23 30
W 6 13 20 27 ..	W 3 10 17 24 ..
T 7 14 21 28 ..	T 4 11 18 25 ..
F 1 8 15 22 29 ..	F 5 12 19 26 ..
S 2 9 16 23 30 ..	S 6 13 20 27 ..

JULY	AUGUST
S .. 5 12 19 26	S 2 9 16 23 30
M - 6 13 20 27	M 3 10 17 24 31
T - 7 14 21 28	T 4 11 18 25 ..
W 1 8 15 22 29	W 5 12 19 26 ..
T 2 9 16 23 30	T 6 13 20 27 ..
F 3 10 17 24 31	F 7 14 21 28 ..
S 4 11 18 25 ..	S 1 8 15 22 29

SEPTEMBER	OCTOBER
S .. 6 13 20 27	S .. 4 11 18 25
M - 7 14 21 28	M - 5 12 19 26
T 1 8 15 22 29	T - 6 13 20 27
W 2 9 16 23 30	W - 7 14 21 28
T 3 10 17 24 ..	T 1 8 15 22 29
F 4 11 18 25 ..	F 2 9 16 23 30
S 5 12 19 20 ..	S 3 10 17 24 31

NOVEMBER	DECEMBER
S 1 8 15 22 29	S .. 6 13 20 27
M 2 9 16 23 30	M - 7 14 21 28
T 3 10 17 24 ..	T 1 8 15 22 29
W 4 11 18 25 ..	W 2 9 16 23 30
T 5 12 19 26 ..	T 3 10 17 24 31
F 6 13 20 27 ..	F 4 11 18 25 ..
S 7 14 21 28 ..	S 5 12 19 26 ..

Calendar
1891

Marry when the year is new,
Always loving, kind, and true.

When February birds do mate
You may wed, nor dread your fate.

If you wed when March winds blow,
Joy and sorrow both you'll know.

Marry in April when you can,
Joy for maiden and for man.

Marry in the month of May,
You will surely rue the day.

Marry when June roses blow,
Over land and sea you'll go.

They who in July do wed
Must labor always for their bread.

Whoever wed in August be,
Many a change are sure to see.

Marry in September's shine,
Your living will be rich and fine.

If in October you do marry,
Love will come, but riches tarry.

If you wed in bleak November
Only joy will come, remember.

When December's snows fall fast,
Marry, and true love will last.

—Ellye Howell Glover
"Dame Curtsey's" Book
of Novel Entertainments
for Every Day in the Year
1907

There is a tender light in the April world more typical of the delicate intimacy of souls, which is the true nearness of the married state, than the passion and joyousness of June.

—*The Ideas of a Plain Country Woman*
1908

As for the days in the week, the following jingle is almost as old as time. Every girl reads it and then of course chooses the day that best suits her convenience.

> Monday for health,
> Tuesday for wealth,
> Wednesday the best day of all;
> Thursday for losses,
> Friday for crosses,
> And Saturday no luck at all.

—Ellye Howell Glover
*"Dame Curtsey's" Book
of Novel Entertainments
for Every Day in the Year*
1907

All other days of the week save Sunday are favored, but she is a plucky bride indeed who would dare face the awful penalties that superstition attaches to a Friday wedding.

—Christine Terhune Herrick
The Modern Hostess
1908

Marriage Ceremony,

First Congregational Church, New London, Conn,

Thursday, Evening, October 7th,

AT EIGHT O'CLOCK.

Mary E. Douglas.

Charles E. Huntington.

Marriage Ceremony, Private,

Tuesday, Jan. 17th, 1882.

Emma Schaerer.

Fred. Baumann.

Married in gray, you will go far away.
Married in black, you will wish yourself back.
Married in brown, you will live out of town.
Married in red, you will wish yourself dead.
Married in pearl, you will live in a whirl.
Married in green, ashamed to be seen.
Married in yellow, ashamed of your fellow.
Married in blue, he will always be true.
Married in pink, your spirits will sink.
Married in white, you have chosen aright.

—Ellye Howell Glover
"Dame Curtsey's" Book of
Novel Entertainments
for Every Day in the Year
1907

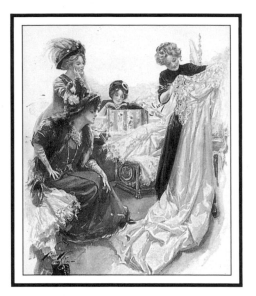

The bride's outfit when she leaves her father's house is very complete, because she will not any longer send her bills to her father or ask him for money to buy clothes.

—Margaret E. Sangster
Good Manners for All Occasions
1904

PERLEY B. MANSFIELD,
DEALER IN
Hats, Caps, Furs, Gloves and Umbrellas
Established 1830.   No. 89 Munroe St., Lynn.

The bridegroom's family, his mother and sisters, are supposed to see that he discards his old clothes of which the best of men are fond, and starts, newly equipped, on his new chapter of life.

—Margaret E. Sangster
Good Manners for All Occasions
1904

It has become very much the fashion in America to follow the English precedent in selecting the hour for the ceremony. Consequently, "high noon" is the more generally selected hour. The origin of this custom in England is not at all flattering to the people of that day, for that early hour, comparatively speaking, had become an absolute necessity if it was desired to insure the sobriety of the bridegroom.

—Christine Terhune Herrick
The Modern Hostess
1908

This is to Certify

That Abner Richardson Mott of Ware in the **STATE** of Massachusetts and Sophronia Cordelia Gibbs of New Salem in the **STATE** of Massachusetts were, by me Joined together in

HOLY MATRIMONY

on the eighth day of February in the Year of our Lord

Witness John E. Mott 1864 William Gordon

Benjamin H. Marsh Minister of the M. E. Church

Just as the naive little wild flower at the old oak's knee is infinitely sweeter and more gifted with spirit than any hothouse rose, so your little wedding has a delicate charm that is smothered in the elaborate details of the rich and extravagant wedding—though both couples may love and love sincerely.

—*The Ideas of a Plain Country Woman*
1908

The sentimental young woman who puts a bit of the wedding cake under her pillow may have a dream that will bring her good fortune.

—Margaret E. Sangster
Good Manners for All Occasions
1904

The bride usually enters on Lohengrin and goes out on Mendelssohn.

—Lillian Eichler
Book of Etiquette
1922

The bride, above all, must not reach up and wig-wag signals while she is receiving, any more than she must wave to people as she goes up and down the aisle of the church. She must not cling to her husband, stand pigeon-toed, or lean against him or the wall, or any person or thing. She must not run her arm through his and let her hand flop on the other side; she must not swing her arms as though they were dangling rope; she must not switch herself this way and that, nor must she "hello" or shout.

—Emily Post
Etiquette
1922

A token of affection.

Tokens
and Toasts

Wedding presents have now become almost absurdly gorgeous. The old fashion, which was started among the frugal Dutch, of giving the young couple their household gear and a sum of money with which to begin, has now degenerated into a very bold display of wealth and ostentatious generosity, so that friends of moderate means are afraid to send anything.

—Mrs. John Sherwood
Manners and Social Usage
1884

A GIFT for
THE HAPPY BRIDAL PAIR!

WEDDING ANNIVERSARIES

First Year—Paper
Second Year—Cotton
Third Year—Leather
Fifth Year—Wood
Seventh Year—Woolens
Tenth Year—Tin
Twelfth Year—Linen
Fifteenth Year—Crystal
Twentieth Year—China
Twenty-fifth Year—Silver
Thirtieth Year—Pearl
Fortieth Year—Ruby
Fiftieth Year—Gold
Seventy-fifth Year—Diamond

—Ellye Howell Glover
"Dame Curtsey's" Book
of Novel Entertainments
for Every Day in the Year
1907

With Best Wishes for The Bride

May you always be happy,
And live at your ease;
Get a kind husband,
And do as you please.

—J. S. Ogilvie
The Album Writer's Friend
1881

The bride's health is drunk standing, after which each man breaks his glass, ostensibly that it may never be put to less honorable use.

—Christine Terhune Herrick
The Modern Hostess
1908

To marriage: The happy state which resembles a pair of shears; so joined that they cannot be separated; often moving in opposite directions, yet always punishing anyone who comes between them.

—*Prosit: A Book of Toasts*
Compiled by Clotho
1904

Happily

Ever After

We have been asked to define the meaning of the word "honey-moon." It comes from the Germans, who drank mead, or metheglin—a beverage made of honey—for thirty days after the wedding.

—Mrs. John Sherwood
Manners and Social Usage
1884

The honey-moon in our busy land is usually only a fortnight in the sky.

—Mrs. John Sherwood
Manners and Social Usage
1884

Some learned authorities declare that the honeymoon is a survival of the primal marriage by capture, when the original cave-man kept his wife in retirement to prevent her from appealing to her relatives for aid.

—Frederick H. Martens
The Book of Good Manners
1923

By a home, we mean a place in which the mind can settle; where it is too much at ease to be inclined to rove; a refuge to which we flee in the expectation of finding those calm pleasures, those soothing kindnesses, which are the sweetness of life.

—Reverend James Bean
Affectionate Advise to a Married Couple
circa 1850

Like a suit at chancery, marriage is likely to last a lifetime; each is much easier to get into than get out of again.

—Frederick Saunders
Salad for the Solitary and the Social
1871

It seems fitting that a book about traditions of the past should be decorated with period artwork. In that spirit, the art in *I Thee Wed* has been taken from personal collections of original nineteenth- and early-twentieth-century calling cards, valentines, wedding invitations, wedding certificates, etchings, postcards, and other paper treasures of the time.

The endpapers and chapter openings contain patterns reproduced from some of our favorite vintage wallpapers.